NOTED WITH THANKS.

Wayn !

WORK-LIFE
BALANCE

Published by
**DIFFERENCE
ENGINE**

Work

Life

Balance

**MALEVOLENT
MANAGERS**

and

**FOLKLORIC
FREELANCERS**

By

**BENJAMIN
CHEE**

and

**WAYNE
RÉE**

CREATORS: BENJAMIN CHEE AND WAYNE RÉE
EDITOR: SHREYA DAVIES | DESIGNER: YONG WEN YEU | MARKETING: MELESA WONG
BUSINESS DEVELOPMENT: CHARLENE SHEPHERDSON | PUBLISHER: FELICIA LOW-JIMENEZ

NATIONAL LIBRARY BOARD, SINGAPORE CATALOGUING IN PUBLICATION DATA
NAME(S) : RÉE, WAYNE. | CHEE, BENJAMIN (CARTOONIST), ILLUSTRATOR.
TITLE : WORK-LIFE BALANCE / WAYNE RÉE, BENJAMIN CHEE.
DESCRIPTION : FIRST EDITION. | SINGAPORE : DIFFERENCE ENGINE, 2022.
IDENTIFIER(S) : ISBN 978-981-18-4559-8 (PAPERBACK) | 978-981-18-4560-4 (EBOOK)
SUBJECT(S) : LCSH : WORK--FICTION. | PARANORMAL FICTION. | WORK--
COMIC BOOKS, STRIPS, ETC. | SUPERNATURAL--COMIC BOOKS, STRIPS, ETC.
CLASSIFICATION : DDC S823--DC23

PRINTED IN SINGAPORE (FIRST EDITION, OCTOBER 2022)
10 9 8 7 6 5 4 3 2 1

DIFFERENCE ENGINE: POWERED BY COMICS
284 RIVER VALLEY ROAD, SINGAPORE 238325
WWW.DIFFERENCEENGINE.SG

Insights, Synergy, & Other Monstrously Empty Buzzwords

A QUICK INTRODUCTION TO THE FORMAT OF WORK-LIFE BALANCE

The easiest way to describe the book you hold in your hands is to call it a prose/comics mash-up — but even that's simplifying things.

It might help to give you a little bit of history as to how the illustrious Benjamin Chee and I got here. Many moons ago, Ben approached me about turning one of my prose short stories — *Mr Memphis*, a supernatural yarn set in the wild west — into a comic. He wanted to do more than just adapt it though. He wanted to keep the old-timey western dialogue, but visualise it in a more wuxia-inspired setting.

It turned out absolutely wonderful, so much so that I simply can't separate the short story from the comic anymore. Yeah, the dialogue and the visuals expertly danced back and forth between contrasting and complementing each other, but the real mastery was in how much Ben reworked the story to fit the comics medium — and, by doing so, made it all his own.

Work-Life Balance is the natural next step from that.

The concept's basically the same: similar stories told across two different genres and two different mediums — office satire in prose, fantastical fables in comics, broadly speaking. This time, however, while the prose and the comics start from the same ideas, we've given ourselves even more freedom to branch off further away from each other.

I used to say that Ben didn't adapt *Mr Memphis*; he remixed it. With *Work-Life Balance*, however, what we're doing is having a conversation with each other. There are elements in the comics inspired by the prose, but likewise, there are parts of the prose that are inspired by things that Ben had done in the comics.

Got all that? Cool. Now, switch off your email notifications, tell your supervisor you'll get back to them later — and let's begin.

— WAYNE RÉE

PRELUDE

Everyone knows about the fight between good and evil.

It's ravaged across tribes, countries, worlds and time. It's sent ripples across whole universes, all so very different from each other in so many ways...

...but also, more alike than you might suspect.

CHAPTER ONE

Take Over

Zee was seven when they first saw their father kill a pontianak.

A young man named Hong had arrived at their Seletar Estate home on a Thursday evening — just another in a long line of visitors that Zee's father would receive seemingly every other night. Normally, their father — a towering figure with rough, sun-kissed brown skin and lines carved into his perpetually scowling face — would shoo Zee and their sister, Sulaiha, into one of the bedrooms, then lock the door from the outside. On this particular evening, however, he only waved Su into the room. He didn't outright ask Zee to join him, but when he offered the visitor a seat, he quietly ordered Zee to make three cups of coffee.

As Zee returned to the living room, precariously carrying the three piping hot cups, they heard Hong speaking, shakily. "My brother didn't deserve that, Uncle. He was a good man, you know? A good man..."

Zee's father asked Hong why he'd come to him instead of letting the police handle the matter. The young man's eyes quickly darted to Zee, then back to their father. Their father only nodded slightly.

"The way it... his stomach... all ripped out like that?" Hong stammered, his eyes still darting back to Zee, despite their father's reassurance. Hong took a deep breath, then continued, his tone angrier, more assertive, while barely hiding a hint of uncertainty and fear. "A man couldn't do that."

Zee's father patted the young man on his shoulder and promised him that he'd make it right. He asked for a few more details, then escorted him out, the visitor's coffee left untouched.

A couple of nights after, Zee's father and two of their uncles took them out to a forested area near Punggol. There, the four of them—all barefoot, but dressed in dark trousers and short-sleeved shirts — waited, hidden within a row of bushes, their faces only faintly illuminated by the light of the full moon. Zee's father and uncles didn't say a word the whole time, and Zee knew better than to ask what was going on. They had always known on some level what their father did. Not his day job—running his own convenience store, just a stone's throw away from their home—but what he did for those visitors that would come at night.

Of course they'd caught snippets of conversations through the bedroom door, but they'd always turned away after a while. It wasn't just because Su would tug on their arm, their younger sister's sense of isolation elevated when her sibling ignored her to listen in on their father's dealings. It wasn't even the gory details, or the mention of the creatures and spirits that their father hunted, that would make Zee flinch. It was the anger in the visitors' voices, the hatred.

As midnight grew closer, stray dogs from all around began to howl. Zee knew the stories and the myths, but was still surprised when they caught a whiff of frangipani. The younger of their two uncles stood up suddenly, walked out onto a dirt path close to where they were hidden and stumbled around, as if he was drunk. He started slurring in Bahasa Melayu, loudly boasting of fights won and sexual conquests, and then stopped to urinate against the trunk of a banana tree.

The frangipani smell grew stronger, but began to sour. As it turned into something resembling the stench of rotting meat, Zee noticed that the banana tree started to shake, gently at first, then more and more violently. From within its leaves emerged a figure, crawling headfirst slowly, deliberately down the trunk like a spider. Its straight, black hair covered its face. Its otherwise pristinely white dress and its long nails were marred with the unmistakable dirty brown of dried blood.

As it snarled and reached for Zee's younger uncle, their father and older uncle leapt out. Their uncles grabbed the pontianak by its arms and pushed it down onto its knees, while their father reached into a large pouch he had slung around his shoulder, and pulled out a hammer and nail.

"Nak!" their father shouted for Zee above the sounds of the creature's shrieks. "Nak, mari ke sini!" Zee quickly stepped out of the bushes and jogged towards their father. Their father explained to them that the only way to stop a pontianak was to drive a nail into a hole at the nape of its neck, turning the creature into an ordinary woman. Their father forcefully pulled its hair aside to show Zee the back of its neck, then ordered them to stand before it, so that they could see the transformation for themselves. Hesitantly, Zee moved to about a metre and a half in front of the creature, but their father yelled at them to get closer, to see the look in its eyes, to see the hatred and anger.

Zee shakily took two steps forward, but saw neither of those things. Under the pontianak's protesting hisses and snarls, what they saw in her eyes instead was fear and a doomed sense of finality — the look of someone who knew that their fate was sealed, but was somehow, at long last, at peace.

Their father drove the nail down into her neck, then pulled out an ornately decorated kris from his pouch — and slit her throat.

The following night, Hong returned to Zee's home. Elated this time instead of uneasy, he shook Zee's father's hand enthusiastically, before handing over an ang pao, thick with notes.

The young man wasn't alone. Behind him stood a nervous, slightly younger woman. Her plainly styled hair was shoulder length and obscured half her face. He introduced her as his sister-in-law, his brother's widow. Hong started going on and on about how the pontianak got what it deserved, how his brother was finally avenged.

Zee, however, had stopped paying attention to him the moment they noticed that the woman's hair strategically hid a large bruise under her left eye.

Zee's father had one more visitor that night, after Hong had left — a peculiar man in a subdued red suit with a matching tie and a deep black shirt, who sounded somewhat German. Zee found it hard to completely focus on the man though, almost as if he constantly sat on their periphery.

This new visitor and Zee's father spoke about things stranger than creatures and spirits — things like "expansions," "mergers" and "shared profits." The peculiar man promised Zee's father that he would return eventually, years down the road — "when conditions were suitable," he had said — and they could talk more then.

Conditions, however, never seemed to be suitable for the man — at least not before Zee's father died ten years later.

❄ ❄ ❄

Lita found it harder and harder to hide at night. She'd been working in Singapore for ten years and couldn't believe how much things had changed in that time, with fewer trees, taller buildings and brighter lights all around. It's not that she even wanted to fall back on her old ways — though she had to admit that she had missed spreading her wings — but she'd worked for only two families, and had barely seen a pay raise in the last decade.

It started with other helpers in the neighbourhood, pleading with her to frighten their more lecherous employers — those family men with wandering eyes and groping hands. She'd even killed a few of them — it's not like she didn't have blood on her hands from back in Capiz, after all — but she'd always made sure that they really deserved it, that these men had gone well beyond leering glances and degrading touches.

The other helpers would pay her — not very much, considering what they were asking her to do, but Lita never asked for more, no matter how much she needed the money. She'd go home that night and, when the family she worked for was fast asleep, she'd sneak up to the housing block's rooftop.

There, she'd remove her clothes, before letting the flesh from her upper back stretch out — framed against thin, barely visible bones, taking a form that only slightly resembled the leathery wings her kind were often portrayed with in movies and on schlocky paperback covers. Lita liked that part. It felt like straightening up after hunching over all day.

She hated what came next though, but only because it would be preceded by a wave of nausea. The flesh from her waist would split apart, allowing her torso to lift up from the rest of her body. Her entrails dripped blood onto the rooftop, blood that she'd have to clean up when she returned before dawn.

Riding the night wind, she'd fly above the growing number of buildings, higher than the lights of the city could reach, until she found the men that she was looking for.

There was a time when she'd make three or four such visits a night. Back then, it wasn't just other helpers looking for her aid, but some of their employers too — Singaporean women abandoned by their husbands. Those times, however, were fading. Her kind had always been hunted, but as this country grew from a plucky developing nation into a perpetually buzzing metropolis, her nightly outings became increasingly more difficult.

Which was why, on this particular night, as she returned in those twilight hours just before the start of a new day, Lita wasn't entirely surprised to find what looked like a hunter waiting for her on the housing block rooftop, beside the lower half of her body. She was surprised, however, by how young they looked — their sharp, dark brown face, framed against wavy shoulder-length hair.

Decked in a crisp, pink batik shirt — with a bamboo orchid pinned below their left collar — and a flowing orange sarong, the hunter twirled an ornately decorated kris in their right hand. There was something... different about this one, Lita noted. Their composed demeanour and colourful style stood in contrast to those who had hounded her and her kind over the last century or so. Even as she screeched at them to step away from the rest of her unclothed body, the hunter hefted their weapon in a manner that seemed to suggest that they were holding it more for their own protection than to attack.

As the flesh along Lita's waist stitched itself together and her wings furled back up against her shoulder blades, the hunter sheathed their kris and, with a warm smile, handed her the denim cutoffs and plain white top she'd been wearing earlier. "What do you want?" Lita asked, her eyes still locked on them as she got dressed.

"To make amends," they responded.

❀ ❀ ❀

No one was ever sure if they had the right address.

The structure looked like a cross between a temple of some kind and a rundown shopfront. It was located around the corner from Raffles Place MRT station, sitting defiantly in prime Central Business District real estate, almost as an affront to the clean, coldly modern steel-and-glass giants that surrounded it. A couple of developers had offered to buy the whole plot of land from Zee, which included a lush garden out back, but Zee — now in their mid-twenties — politely refused. Some of those developers grew pushier, but within a matter of days they had rescinded their demands — pale-faced, paranoid and profusely apologetic.

The structure housed a large, sparsely furnished space. Its dull grey concrete floors looked like they had never seen a broom. In the middle sat a wobbly round table with two red plastic seats on either side, donated to Zee by a grateful coffee shop auntie who'd asked them if they could scare off the loan sharks that had been harassing her. The space didn't need much else, Zee felt. After all, this was just a place for them to meet their clients, a conveniently located office of sorts, so that no matter who needed their help, they'd always be about thirty minutes away.

It was dusk on a Monday evening, when a tall woman in her early thirties, sporting an office-friendly black skirt and beige blouse, knocked on the plain wooden door. "Hello?" she ventured, taking a hesitant step in.

"Rubyni, yes?" said Zee, standing up and welcoming the woman in, gesturing towards the seat across from them. "We spoke on the phone last week."

She nodded and entered, still looking around the mostly empty space suspiciously, but noting with a slight smile how much she appreciated the boldness of Zee's blue batik shirt and pink sarong ensemble. Like all of Zee's clients, she'd heard about them from a friend of a friend — the hushed whispers of someone who could solve problems that others didn't even want to talk about.

Zee asked her what had brought her to them, but despite their calm, reassuring tone, the woman dithered and fidgeted on the plastic seat, her lips curled up awkwardly. Zee grinned mirthlessly, recognising the wariness. They'd seen some variation of it from almost all their clients and eventually came to understand that it wasn't just their peculiar line of work that inspired that response; it was also the years and years of their clients feeling dismissed and waved off by the very people that they thought would help.

Adjusting themselves, so that they faced Rubyni more directly, Zee said, accentuating the sincerity in their tone as best they could, "All right, how about this?" Rubyni's fidgeting gradually died down as Zee continued speaking. "You tell me what the problem is, and I'll tell you — and show you — what we can do. If you're still not convinced after that, then clearly I'm not the person for you. Does that sound fair?"

Rubyni paused, her brow furrowed in thought, before her expression eased up a little. Her lips curled up again, this time in a tight smile. "It does."

She inhaled, her smile giving way to a look of steely resolve that barely hid the frustration bubbling beneath. Zee recognised that from a lot of their other clients too. "I have a younger cousin. Matthew," Rubyni began. "He's not like his brothers. He's not like his father. He's... well, he's more... sensitive, you understand?" Zee, of course, knew what she meant. "He's been bullied since he was a kid and I've tried to be there for him, even when the rest of his family or his school wouldn't. Since he entered junior college though, the bullying's only gotten worse."

She paused again, that frustration showing just a little more. "I've seen the bruises that he tries to hide from me. I'm worried that these other boys," she said, practically spitting out that last word, "they're going to take things too far with him."

Rubyni exhaled a breath she hadn't realised she'd been holding, then continued, her tone more level. "I... look, you *seem* like a good person, so if this is some scam or trick, please just let me know now. Please. Matthew doesn't deserve..."

Zee waited a moment as Rubyni trailed off, then let out another breath. "Let me tell you why I do what I do," they said finally. "Aside from my sister, most of my family was a lot like yours when I was growing up. I never could be what they expected because, like Matthew, it just isn't who I am. I learned that very, very early on." They stopped for just a second — the memory of that night along the dirt road in Punggol, as always, hitting them like a punch to the gut — then continued, "My father was not a good man. He hurt people that were different for a living — and he wanted me to do the same. When he died, I thought I'd never enter the family business, that I'd leave his world behind."

Zee extended their hand towards Rubyni. She hesitated for a second, but saw the look in their eyes, then placed her hand in theirs. Together, they stood up and made their way towards a door in the back, the one that led out to the garden.

"I spoke to some of the kinds of people that my father had hurt, and I realised that I couldn't just leave his world behind," they said, before opening the door. "I needed to make it better. I needed to give those people an... outlet to be who they truly are."

The garden was filled with rows of banana trees, many of them taller than even the structure itself. Beneath the trees were all manner of jars and urns. On a stone bench in the corner of the garden, Lita sat languidly in a white t-shirt and light blue jeans, absently flipping through a magazine under the light of the moon, as her flip-flops dangled lazily off her feet. When the door opened, she sat up straight and offered a smile for Rubyni and a nod for Zee. She placed her magazine down on the bench, then lifted a bamboo drum up from the ground onto her lap and played a slow, almost hypnotic rhythm.

"Whatever happens," Zee said to Rubyni, "don't worry, all right?" More confused than frightened, she could only manage a quiet, "Mm," in response. Zee then turned towards the trees and chanted in a language that sounded to Rubyni a little like Bahasa Melayu, but... older.

The air on this Monday evening was still, but the leaves of every tree suddenly began to rustle, then shake furiously, just as Rubyni caught the sweet scent of frangipani. Childlike giggles echoed against the stone walls that shielded the garden from the bustling city beyond, and shadows moved within shadows. From the restless leaves, women started to crawl down like spiders. Some of them wore stained white dresses and had straight, black hair that obscured their faces. Others had porcelain pale skin and bright red lips, with matching red dresses and rickety umbrellas under their arms. From within the jars and urns, unnervingly small children with sickly green skin and sharp teeth emerged, running playfully around the foot of the trees. Just beyond these trees, the shadows began to dance, as more and more creatures — things of myth and nightmare — came forward into the light.

Overwhelmed, Rubyni's eyes darted back and forth, unsure of how to process the enormity of what lay before her. She turned to Lita, hoping to find some anchor to normalcy, but realised that the drumbeat had stopped, only a second before she saw that the woman's now bare light brown upper body had separated from its naked lower half.

Rubyni felt a gasp catch in her throat, but Zee squeezed her hand reassuringly. She turned back towards them and realised, much to her surprise, that she still wasn't frightened. In fact, if anything, she was filled with a sense of awe, of kinship on an almost primal level.

"If you still want our help," Zee said, with a decidedly cheekier grin, "I can guarantee that those boys are never gonna bother Matthew ever again."

That Tuesday, after school, had been like any other.

No matter what plan of escape or strategy Matthew had formulated throughout the day, his tormentors — three seniors named Joshua, Kevin and Nicholas — would always find him. This time, they'd cornered him behind the canteen. Like the countless times before, he'd tried to reason with them first, tried to find some deeper meaning behind why they constantly picked on him. When they only responded with hurtful, venomous insults about his sexuality, Matthew, as always, would call them cowards.

That first punch to the gut was always the worst because he never knew which of the three would deliver it. After they pushed him down to the ground, and started stomping on him — laughing, as they left dirty shoe prints against his otherwise pristinely white school uniform — he could at least close his eyes and pretend he was somewhere else or, on those really bad days, someone else.

The following day, after school, the seniors cornered Matthew again. This time, however, they came to him not with maliciously eager smirks and spiteful words — but pale-faced, paranoid and profusely apologetic. Tears in their eyes, they sobbed and pleaded for forgiveness. At that moment, Matthew felt more confused than anything else.

That night, however, while recounting the bullies' bizarre change of heart to his cousin Rubyni over the phone, it finally hit him. Maybe it was the overwhelming relief in Rubyni's voice, but he knew, with all his heart, that this wasn't some ploy or trick. He was free — finally free — of their hatred... and things could only get better now.

Mephistopheles watched Rubyni leave with a smile on her face and a lightness in her step that she hadn't had just a few evenings ago. Dressed in a sharp red suit with a matching tie and black shirt, he was sitting at a newly opened international coffeehouse down the street from Zee's office. As he sipped his drink — around five times the price of a similar cup at a local coffee shop or kopitiam — the demon thought about how his superiors at The Company couldn't have picked a better country for their Southeast Asian headquarters. The conditions here were, finally, just right.

In fact, most local practitioners of the otherworldly arts had already sold their businesses to The Company. The multinational had approached them under the guise of being a global organisation dedicated to furthering supernatural defence, which was a flimsy ruse at best, but these demons still had enough power on this plane to cloud people's minds, at least a little.

The truth was that they didn't want to risk the competition, either for or against their end goal — the ultimate end goal of a company formed and run by demons of a more apocalyptic nature.

Zee, however, was the one holdout. Mephistopheles genuinely admired them. He wished he'd still had that kind of will — and stubbornness — but he'd run afoul of the upper hierarchies too many times before. Any further rebellion and trickery on his part would only earn him a more severe reprimanding than being demoted to a lower level demon. As far as he had fallen off the corporate ladder though, Mephistopheles knew that he was still their best dealmaker — and, more importantly, they knew it too.

Mammon and Belial had tried to talk to Zee the month before. The pair offered them wealth and fortune — the standard deal-with-a-devil fare — and to take Zee's "vision to new heights," a line that filled Mephistopheles with no small amount of second-hand embarrassment. For their troubles, Mammon and Belial were tossed out of Zee's space by a mountainous rākṣasī named Tashny.

Mephistopheles decided to take another approach: honesty — or his version of it, at least.

Knocking on Zee's door, the demon introduced himself immediately as a representative of The Company. Zee didn't invite him in. They barely even looked up from their newspaper, and only acknowledged him with a "Hmm?" and a raised, manicured eyebrow.

"I know that my colleagues have already spoken to you," Mephistopheles said. "But I was hoping to give it one more try."

"And what do you think you can say that will convince me, demon?" Zee said, still not looking at him.

"Your time has faded," he replied, his German accent suddenly more pronounced — but only slightly and only just enough.

That got Zee's attention. They put the newspaper down and spat, "Has it now?"

"I know you do this as much for them," Mephistopheles said, tilting his chin towards the door at the back, "as for the people who come to you for help. And you've built a nice, safe space for them here. Safe working conditions too, safe enough for them to never run into men... like your father."

Zee balled up their fist. They didn't seem conscious of this. Mephistopheles, however, was. "How many visitors did he get every night — and how many do you get?" he continued. "Belief in your little pack back there is waning. It has been since the eighties, since these big ol' buildings started popping up faster than ever. And we should know. The Company has been keeping track of this since then, and a whole lot longer. So, how many more people like Rubyni are going to come to you with their problems, giving your monsters a means to be who they are?"

Zee held a glare at Mephistopheles for a moment, before they unclenched their fist and slumped into a contemplative slouch. They thought back to the night they had met Lita. She had told them as much — that her kind were past their prime — but Zee's desire to undo their father's wrongs had overshadowed all of that.

"To make amends," they had told her. But maybe the haunting memory of their father's sins — made real by the look in that pontianak's eyes — outweighed the actual amount of penance that they expected of themselves.

"I'm not going to feed you a line of bullshit," Mephistopheles said, shaking Zee out of their thoughts. "You can clearly see through all of that. But you also know that The Company can provide them with as close to a safe space as possible, as this country moves into a new era."

Mephistopheles ventured a few more steps into the space, and placed a matte black name card onto the wobbly round table. He held Zee's gaze for a second, keeping his expression completely neutral, then said, "I'll see myself out." The demon turned around and slowly headed back the way he came in.

Zee, however, stopped him before he could step out into the street. "Do I know you from somewhere?" they said.

Mephistopheles allowed himself a slight grin. Without turning around or missing a beat, he replied, plainly, "Not at all."

❄ ❄ ❄

"Titi Zee!" Dina shouted. Zee's niece — Sulaiha's daughter — ran into their arms. She was so excited to see them that she didn't even notice when her pistachio ice cream plopped off its cone and onto the Central Business District pavement.

"Hello, sayang!" Zee said, lifting the seven-year-old off the ground and spinning her around. "My goodness, you've grown so much!"

"She has seriously missed her Titi Zee," said Su's husband, Suresh, with a hearty chuckle and a brotherly grin plastered across his face, as he gently patted Zee on their back.

"We all have," said Su, keeping her distance a little more than her husband, but still unable to conceal the wistfulness in her voice.

"I know," Zee said, sadly at first, then continuing with a more upbeat tone, as much for Dina as for their sister and brother-in-law, "but Titi Zee's done with all the work that's been keeping them busy, and they can promise that they'll be around more these days."

"I can play the violin now, you know, Titi Zee?" Dina said, as the family headed to a nearby café.

"Is that... so?" Zee said, trailing off a little as they passed a newly constructed office tower, just around the corner from Raffles Place MRT station. At the entrance, Zee saw Lita — now sporting a pantsuit and professional white blouse — smoking and staring longingly at the sky.

Almost as if drawn by their glare, she turned towards Zee, and offered a tight, melancholic smile. Zee furrowed their brow — trying to say to her with just a look all the things that they had left unsaid for the last two years, all the choices that they wished they had the power to make, all the regrets that weren't theirs to carry.

She seemed to understand though, her smile widening a little as she gave them that familiar nod that they had grown so fond of over nearly a decade.

Exhaling a breath that they didn't know they were holding in, Zee turned to their sister. She immediately recognised the whirlwind of emotions that this particular building worked up in her sibling, even if she didn't understand exactly why. She'd seen it before in their eyes — many times, years ago, in their Seletar Estate home. She took her sibling's hand and held it in hers, as they turned another corner and reached their destination.

Suresh held the café's door open, gesturing for Su and Zee to walk through, truly together for the first time in a long time.

HE HURT PEOPLE THAT WERE *DIFFERENT* FOR A LIVING ...

...AND HE WANTED *ME* TO DO THE SAME.

WHEN HE DIED...

...I THOUGHT I'D NEVER ENTER THE *FAMILY BUSINESS.*

THAT I'D LEAVE HIS WORLD BEHIND.

Work-Life Balance

Curious.

I haven't heard anything *good* about your Company.

That is unfortunate.

We'll be sure to evaluate our employees' performance,

and make sure your experience with us is *satisfying*.

In the meantime, let's go back to these terms.

Our standard offer entails wealth beyond mea—

Actually,

if you did *take over* my business...

Work-Life Balance

I CANNOT JUST LEAVE MY FATHER'S WORLD BEHIND.

I NEED TO MAKE IT BETTER.

I NEED TO GIVE THEM AN...

...OUTLET TO BE WHO THEY TRULY ARE.

Work-Life Balance

Not today.

Not while we still have customers who need our help.

Speaking of which,

Madam Rubyni replies that she will be here in the evening,

on behalf of her young cousin.

I *NEED* TO GIVE THEM AN OUTLET TO BE WHO THEY TRULY ARE.

Great, I'll be expecting her.

TO PROTECT THOSE OF US WHO
DON'T YET HAVE THE STRENGTH...

...AND KEEP IT GOING FOR AS LONG AS I CAN.

Work-Life Balance

Take Over

Work-Life Balance

CHAPTER TWO

Hearsay

I t was eight forty-five on a Tuesday morning. The demon from middle-management was waiting in a corner of the foyer, his hands casually crossed behind his back. His overall demeanour, likewise, seemed aloof, but his striking red suit and tie, coupled with his bold black shirt, ensured that he stood out among the foyer's simple design.

The Company's ground floor sported floor-to-ceiling windows, and a marble reception counter, with two elevators behind it, each accessible only with a specially coded keycard. There were no ornate statues or sculptures, no waiting area with comfortable sofas or coffee tables adorned with months-old magazines. No human visited The Company's office — not unless they had dealings with the demons that ran it.

The receptionist — a pontianak named Tiqqy, with long, flowing hair, wearing an equally flowing flower-print dress — eyed the demon suspiciously. She'd been a part of The Company since they'd taken over the business that she'd previously worked for — and she'd never trusted him. To be fair, it's not like she liked the demons from the upper hierarchies either, but at least they were upfront about their goals. It was right there in The Company's mission statement, after all.

"To acquire the power to destroy civilisation and bring the world to an end."

In the decade that she'd worked here, however, she could never figure out what motivated this particular demon. He never seemed entirely on board with the upper hierarchies' goals. She'd heard rumours that he'd had some sort of falling-out with them ages ago, and had since been relegated to perpetually flounder in his current role, where he couldn't cause any trouble — but where they could still keep him under their thumb.

What Tiqqy did know was that, every time a new addition to The Company arrived on their first day, he'd be there to greet them at the foyer — even though it wasn't a task mandated to him by his superiors, and it never seemed to lead to any obvious machinations on his part.

A kuchisake-onna, newly transferred from The Company's Osaka office, walked through the glass doors, giving a cursory look around the unfurnished foyer, before her attention landed on Tiqqy. Like the pontianak and all the rest of the otherworldly creatures that worked here, the kuchisake-onna disguised herself to look mostly human. The only thing that really set her apart was the face mask that covered her mouth, the kind that had been a rarity in Singapore, but was all too common among well-mannered office workers in Japan at the time. From the sides of the mask, however, Tiqqy could still make out the scabbed-over slits that stretched from the corners of her lips to the middle of her cheeks.

The kuchisake-onna walked purposefully towards the reception counter, her eyes smiling. "Hello," she said, politely upbeat. "My name is Asuka.

It is my first day and—"

Before she could reach the counter, however, the demon from middle-management stepped in from his corner of the foyer. "Hi," he said, a slight German accent hidden under a neutral transatlantic inflection. Tiqqy could never make out his tone. It always seemed disingenuous to her, but she sometimes wondered if that was just because of her own feelings towards him.

The demon reached out his hand, just as Asuka began to bow. They both laughed awkwardly and negotiated what would be an appropriate greeting, before finally settling on a handshake.

"Pleased to meet you," he continued. "My name is Mephistopheles."

❈ ❈ ❈

Kidōmaru, Asuka's supervisor back in Osaka, had assured her before she left that she would be a "valuable member of the Singapore office's administrative division," though with his perpetually stern expression and grunt that punctuated every other sentence, she couldn't be entirely sure that assurance was his intention. And while her revamp of their filing system was undoubtedly a marked improvement, it was never her efficiency that she had doubts about.

Her local supervisor, Xiao Huang — a seemingly youthful woman with a fashion sense that hadn't progressed very much beyond the mid-eighties — tried her best to help Asuka settle in. She'd joined her for lunch those first couple of days, but even when Huang was too busy, she always made sure that Asuka still had company.

Asuka's colleagues were friendly enough, asking about where The Company had put her up or whether she had tried any of the local food or even, bless them, if she wanted to join them for karaoke one of these days. But the harder they tried to help her fit in — going out of their way to make her feel welcome — the more disconnected she felt.

On a Monday afternoon, however, while discreetly nibbling on a stick of chicken satay at Lau Pa Sat, her curiosity got the better of her awkwardness when Lita, a manananggal from her department with a penchant for pantsuits, mentioned Mephistopheles to Tashny, a powerhouse of a rākṣasī from the security division with a closely cropped crew cut, in a tone that dripped with disgust.

"Excuse me for asking," Asuka said, taking Lita and Tashny a little by surprise, despite her slight hesitation, "but what exactly does Mephistopheles... do?"

The manananggal and the rākṣasī exchanged looks for a second, then burst out laughing. Before Asuka's anxiety could get the better of her, however, Lita leaned forward conspiratorially and said, "Oh, ate. We've both been working here for the better part of ten years — and neither of us still knows what Mephistopheles does."

"I've got access to all security files up to middle-management," Tashny said, slowly, her supposed overbite hiding the fangs that grew out of the upper half of her jaw. "His is just... this complete mess," she continued with an exaggerated shrug. "Everything written in there contradicts something else."

Asuka's brow furrowed in confusion. "But why? How?"

"No idea," said Lita. "There are rumours, of course. I've heard a couple of demons say that he's a spy for the upper hierarchies, which really wouldn't surprise me. I can practically smell the duplicity on him."

"Whatever it is," Tashny said, "I wouldn't trust him if I were you, Asuka."

Asuka just smiled and nodded. Mephistopheles had invited her out for lunch a couple of times, but Huang always stepped in, and Asuka supposed that this... ambiguity could be why — but she still wasn't certain that her colleagues' feelings towards him were entirely justified.

She held onto this uncertainty until later, after lunch, as the three of them passed Mephistopheles in the hall. "Hello, Asuka," the demon from middle-management said. He seemed genuine enough, but Asuka's mind raced to what Tashny and Lita had said earlier, and in that moment — and under the watchful, protective eyes of her colleagues — her earlier scepticism began to wilt. She wanted to think better of Mephistopheles, she did.

But she felt so alone here, so far away from home.

She responded with nothing more than a cold half-smile, the slits at the corner of her lips barely curling upwards, then continued on with Lita and Tashny. She thought she'd heard a scoff coming from his direction, but when she glanced back quickly, he was already gone.

※ ※ ※

In her previous life, Xiao Huang had heard men spit all manner of curses at her. It was something that a ba jiao gui got used to very quickly. It wasn't like a jiang shi or a shui gui. Those spirits had it easier — they just went straight for the kill.

Huang and her kind, however, would always give men's better natures a chance first, offering them the right combination of lucky numbers to strike it rich in the lottery. All they had to do was meet this opportunity with gratitude instead of greed.

They almost always chose the latter.

None of those curses that they spat at her, however, as she viciously tore them apart, made her wince quite as much as the word that demons like Mammon and Belial used for drink nights with the upper hierarchies.

Schmoozing.

These nights — initiated a couple of years back by Leviathan to "foster team spirit" — were never made explicitly compulsory, but after thirteen years as part of The Company, Huang knew how things really worked. All the demons from middle-management on up were there at this high-end hotel bar — and if they weren't, then it wouldn't be long before Abaddon brought it up.

Abaddon was part of Mammon and Belial's circle of demons, the ones that sat on the lower rung of the upper hierarchies. They didn't have the same level of power and influence as someone like Leviathan — and Huang knew how that made them feel. She'd seen it in men long before she joined The Company, after all.

And as with those men, these demons chose to work out those feelings of inadequacy on others. After just two shots of vodka, Belial — squat and perpetually sweaty Belial — would boast about how he'd brought Tashny down to his level when he delayed her regular security checks of his department's personnel. Mammon, with his leering eyes and too-long tongue that was seemingly always licking his lips, wouldn't even need a drop of alcohol to brag about how many women from the office — creatures, spirits, and demons alike — he'd added to his little black book of conquests.

On this particular evening, however, Abaddon dominated the conversation with his casual contempt for the absent Mephistopheles — and that certainly caught Huang's attention. She felt no love for Mephistopheles, her fellow creature of middle-management — not since the day he had come to the business that she'd previously worked for, the same business where Tiqqy, Tashny, Lita and so many others had worked. He'd come promising them a safe space, but all they got was a place to hide — Tiqqy's ferocity hidden behind the flower prints of her dresses, Lita's wings hidden beneath the weight of her pantsuits, Tashny's fangs hidden behind her overbite.

Huang's justice against the greed of man — hidden behind the title of Senior Manager of Finance and Administration.

For all this time, when she thought of how homogenised her life had become, the face she saw was Mephistopheles'. But as Abaddon and Belial and Mammon — demons who came to Singapore all those years ago, along with Mephistopheles — laughed at him, called him a powerless underling, a toothless snake in a cheap suit, Huang found herself wondering, for the first time in those thirteen years, if Mephistopheles wasn't part of their ilk either, then who was he really?

·

❄ ❄ ❄

It was a late Sunday evening. Mephistopheles looked out of his Tiong Bahru flat's balcony window, down at the still bustling street below. Older residents who'd lived here most of their lives were picking up dinner at coffee shops that had been around since they first moved in. Younger crowds who visited the neighbourhood only on the weekends, armed with their Polaroid cameras, were heading to the newer bakeries, cafés and pubs, for social media-friendly dishes, desserts and drinks.

Mephistopheles remembered moving in here fifteen years ago, after The Company had officially set up its local office. The neighbourhood was quieter then, but even with all the changes over the years, he could still close his eyes and hear the beating heart of its true spirit just beneath the surface.

He knew about the rumours and the chatter around the office — but he also knew that there was no point in trying to fight them. They'd festered and taken on a life of their own over the years, becoming as much a part of The Company's culture as casual Fridays.

On some level, however, he knew that he'd also earned all the malicious gossip that persisted about him, because there was some truth in all of it. He'd earned it a little over a century ago, when he thought that ambition was what The Company was looking for — but what they really wanted was compliance. He'd earned it when he still tried to play within the system, to try and regain his spot back in the upper hierarchies, by helping The Company gobble up all these smaller businesses — but all that earned him was the ire of the creatures and spirits that they incorporated in their wake, helped along by a suspiciously misplaced personnel file or two; the very creatures and spirits he had hoped to also provide a safe haven for within The Company.

Because he was someone that dealt in half-truths, Mephistopheles was always keenly aware of hard facts — and the fact was that he was trapped in some kind of corporate limbo: a scapegoat that his superiors used to foster a united hatred from his peers.

What's worse was that it was a limbo of his own making. If he had left after he'd initially run afoul with the upper hierarchies, he'd be free of them — but he was too fearful of making it completely on his own, without The Company's backing. He couldn't leave now though; they wouldn't let him, not with his intimate understanding of The Company — and certainly not with whispers of outside forces amassing against them.

He'd earned this, all of this. But that didn't stop him from trying to earn back a shred of dignity, if not his reputation, one person at a time.

The young woman was one of the few humans to ever step through the glass doors of The Company's Singaporean office. They'd been hiring more of them, since the upper hierarchies realised that their expansion was limited with a purely demon-led workforce. They'd initially thought that it would be hard to find humans willing to go along with The Company's mission, but as it turned out, much to their surprise, humans' feelings towards the apocalypse were... complicated.

As always, Mephistopheles stood in his corner — and as always, Tiqqy said nothing, only glancing over at him with disdain, every other minute. He wished he could tell her why he did this — but more than that, he wished that telling her would make a difference.

Every new hire was a chance to change perceptions, a chance to reestablish himself as something other than everyone's adversary. What he didn't even tell himself though was that every new hire was also a chance for him to just make a friend.

"Hi," he said, stepping forward with a smile on his face.

"Uh... hi," said the young woman, taken aback by his enthusiasm, though thankfully not offended or frightened by it. "I'm Dina. It's my first day today."

"Pleased to meet you," he said, hoping she didn't misconstrue the slight quiver in his smile as insincerity. "My name is Mephistopheles."

Pleased to meet you.

Dina sayang,

Titi Zee has to *entertain* a visitor.

Go find your mother, okay?

Yes, Titi Zee.

Work-Life Balance

Work-Life Balance

Safe working conditions too!

Safe enough for them to *never* run into men like your father.

Hearsay

Work-Life Balance

The management took some persuading, but yes.

The Company has *agreed* to prepare a place for *everyone* who works with you...

If they want it.

I know this is important to you.

Well...

I'll see myself out.

Come to think of it,

I did ask them to send someone better.

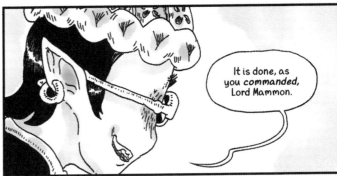

It is done, as you *commanded*, Lord Mammon.

The witchdoctor has sold their business to The Company.

Congratulations are in order, Mephistopheles.

You have accomplished what I *could not*.

Merely a different tack, Lord Belial.

I couldn't have done it on my own,

without your laying the *foundation* for this deal.

HMPH!

Work-Life Balance

Hearsay

Work-Life Balance

Work-Life Balance

I want these files organised and on my desk by tomorrow morning.

Thank you.

Huang!

Congratulations on your promotion!

Thank you.

I haven't seen you two much since we left Zee's.

You must've been busy.

Hearsay

Work-Life Balance

CHAPTER THREE

Wandering Spirit

"Thank you for absolutely nothing," Xiao Huang whispered shakily, her eyes shut. She stood just outside of Belial's office, the tip of her nose barely a few inches from his closed door. If she tried hard enough, she could pick up the stench of his body spray.

Tall, lean and pale, Huang was dressed in a fitting black-and-white dress topped with too-large shoulder pads — her outfit, as always, inspired by the decade in which she had come into being. She continued, "Your consistent lack of ability to provide any useful help is comfortingly predictable."

Her colleagues... well, ex-colleagues now, she supposed — a handful of humans, and a collection of pontianaks, manananggals, rākṣasīs, and other spirits and creatures — stared at her, unsure whether the ba jiao gui was going to barge into Belial's office and disembowel him. More than a few of them — much more than Belial would've expected — secretly hoped she would. Huang smiled mirthlessly. If there was anything about The Company she was going to miss, it was the bonds she had forged and strengthened over the last fifteen years.

With controlled breaths, Huang wondered to herself, not for the first time, how she even managed to last that long in The Company, as a Senior Manager of Finance and Administration. Her decisions were constantly, and smugly, undercut by the demons from the upper hierarchies like Belial — and why? Because, she realised too late in those fifteen years, they simply knew that they could.

The Company did provide her with job security though. Belief in the beyond had waned locally, even before the multinational made Singapore its regional headquarters. But, even as she contemplated whether she wanted to make a scene, Huang realised just how much her time here had affected her, how the weight of the years kept her claws by her side. "I must question why I banged my head against the wall," she said, then sighed, opened her eyes and walked through the maze of cubicles — first, to meet and conduct a handover with her replacement, then towards the exit.

"The fault," she said, "is entirely my own."

❋ ❋ ❋

In the month since she had left The Company, Huang had been approached by just one person — Victor, a dishevelled middle-aged man with a gambling problem whose uncle Huang had slain back in the late eighties. Victor had started out all right, following all the proper customs to call upon a ba jiao gui — tying a red string around the banana tree she lived in, then sticking the tree with needles — but even so, she had her doubts about him when she appeared at the foot of his bed that night.

He had the same uneasy twitch as his uncle, a nervous tic that she'd spotted in so many other men who refused to honour their deal. The man pleaded with her — just one set of lucky lottery numbers to get him out of debt, that's all he asked for. He wouldn't even need all of his winnings, he had said, going so far as to offer her a cut.

Huang hesitated for a moment, the desperation in his tone only deepening her concern, but eventually, she relented. It was not like she was exactly flooded with job offers, after all. So, there at the foot of his bed in a flat nearly devoid of material possessions, she stood, wearing a bright red dress from a time before she came into being — more for effect than for anything else — and carrying an equally old oil-paper umbrella. Her eyes lit up as she radiated within the halo of a cold, blue flame. Above her, she wrote against a canvas of nothing, and where the tip of her umbrella moved, a trail of that flame followed, burning four digits into the air.

Victor cried tears of joy, dancing around at the prospect of getting his life back on track. He promised that, in a week, he would let her go with a quarter of his winnings, the sense of gratitude sending the pitch of his voice higher.

The following week, he asked for another set of numbers.

"That wasn't the deal," Huang said, her voice level. The flames that surrounded her burned brighter than before.

"But it's just one more time," he said, the desperation in his tone replaced by an all-too-familiar arrogance. "What's the harm?"

Huang didn't say anything in response, partly for effect, but partly because she was disappointed — not in him, but in herself. "The fault is entirely my own," she thought, as the flames around her began to rage. Victor reeled in fright from the fires that he feared would set him ablaze.

If he had been smarter, he'd have paid more attention to her claws instead.

Wiping the blood from her hands, Huang was taken aback by a sound she hadn't heard in a while: the beep of an email notification from her phone. Her surprise — and interest — grew as she opened a message from Shao, a jovial monk she had known during her early days.

He had moved to Bangkok in the nineties, but not before he had introduced Huang to Zee, the person she had worked with before The Company. Like Zee, Shao had been her mortal go-between, helping her find clients who genuinely needed the money — and, more importantly, who wouldn't let their greed overpower their better natures. She trusted Shao more than almost any other human, so when he asked her to come to Thailand for a potential job opportunity, she responded almost immediately with, "I'll see you tomorrow afternoon."

Despite how much he'd clearly aged since the last time Huang had seen him, Shao was still a bear of a man. Which was why, when he waved at her with childlike enthusiasm from across the carpark at Suvarnabhumi Airport, she had to stifle a laugh — but then, almost immediately and very suddenly, felt the full force of just how much she had missed him.

Dressed in a white Duran Duran t-shirt, faded blue high-waisted jeans and a pair of ankle-high red sneakers, Huang ran towards Shao — dodging bicycles, motorbikes, cars and crowds — then leapt into his arms. Shao's light grey, loose fitting robes didn't belong to any particular denomination, but still, they exuded an almost infectious tranquillity.

Holding onto the hug for just a little while longer, Huang asked, her voice muffled by the folds of those robes, "So, what's this job you've got for me?" She inhaled deeply before finally letting him go, and was happy to find that, even after all these years, his robes still smelled of lavender.

"It's for a village outside of Kanchanaburi," he said, walking over to the driver's side of what looked like an old military jeep.

"A... village?" Huang said. She involuntarily let out a disappointed sigh, then immediately tried to disguise it as a grunt by hefting her backpack in an almost exaggerated manner. "Look, Shao. I appreciate the message," she said, mindful of her tone. "And it's really great to see you again." She paused. "But I can't just fly to Thailand on the off-chance that someone in a village somewhere could use a set of lucky numbers."

Shao gave her a knowing smile, as he climbed into the jeep. "Who said the village needed a ba jiao gui?"

The sky was milky red, the last lights of the warm day fading as Shao pulled the jeep over to the side of the dirt path that they had been driving down for the better part of the past half-hour. Up ahead, Huang could make out the village itself — a cluster of bamboo huts on stilts built around the same path. On either side of them, and surrounding the village, were forests of banana trees as far as the eye could see.

It hadn't taken long on their approximately two-hour drive for the pair to settle back into comfortable familiarity — small talk bleeding into shared memories, topped off with just a bit of catching up.

About an hour into the ride, however, Huang circled their conversation back, and asked Shao for more details about the job they were heading towards. The monk patiently sidestepped her questions, promising that it'd be easier to explain when they reached the village — so, the second the jeep came to a complete stop, Huang flung the vehicle's creaky passenger door open and hopped out.

"Well, we're here," she said. "Now, you can stop being so mysterious about—" It took her a moment to realise what had happened — and even then, her head was swirling with panic and confusion.

Her sneakers had somehow vanished. Disconcerted by the sudden feel of sand against her soles, she looked down — and discovered that her t-shirt and jeans had changed into a fitting set of traditional pha biang and pha nung, both the colour of the leaves surrounding them.

She twisted the vehicle's side-view mirrors to get a better look at herself, but jumped back in shock. Her complexion was a matching, though slightly lighter shade of green. Her features had altered slightly too, and as she stammered, she realised that her accent seemed closer to the locals' inflection.

"Shao? Shao!" she yelled.

The monk rushed over and quickly grabbed the spirit by her shoulders, steadying her shaking frame. The familiarity of his calloused palms brought some comfort, grounding her in the moment enough for her to finally ask, "What's... what's happening to me?"

"Something that many of your kind learn eventually," Shao said, his tone reassuringly level. "You, the pontianaks, manananggals, rākṣasīs and the rest — you all come from the same place: the minds of weak men, whose greatest fear is that those they try to hold under their power... would wield vicious power of their own. You are their nightmares given form. That makes you as much an idea as you are an entity — ideas that are seen through your eyes, yes, but for some of you, can also be seen through the prism of different cultures."

The spirit thought of her ex-colleagues from The Company, and the other spirits and creatures that Zee had worked with. She thought about the kinship that they had shared, and realised that it had very little to do with their disdain for Belial and his ilk. She thought about how, before they shared cubicle spaces — they had shared banana trees in Zee's garden.

"You already wanted to find yourself when I reached out to you. It's the reason why you're more open to this now," Shao said, holding onto her tighter. "You know you're not just a Senior Manager of Finance and Administration — but you aren't even just a ba jiao gui either." He paused for a moment, then loosened his grip and said, "You've been both of those things, and more — all this time. Because there are so many different ways... of being you."

Her confusion finally giving way to certainty, the spirit said, more to herself than to Shao, "A ba jiao gui to greedy nephews in Singapore is as much a pontianak to vile fathers in Indonesia or Malaysia." Her attention moved to the cluster of huts down the path. "Or even a nang tani to the lecherous husband in this village."

She found herself elevating slightly off the ground, the dirt falling gently from the soles of her feet. It didn't feel like she had transformed into something else. It was like this other entity that she had *always* been... was finally awake.

Shao nodded, then let her shoulders go. "That's right, Huang," he said, the warmth of his knowing smile helping her to completely compose herself.

"Not Huang. Not here," she said, responding with a smile of her own. "Here, I am Nay. And I have a job to do."

That night, as the light of the full moon shined down upon the village, Nay laid in wait among the leaves of a nearby banana tree, eating a serving of mango sticky rice. The dessert had been left for her at the foot of the tree by Mai, a woman in her forties from the village, whom Shao had spoken to a week before.

Before long, Mai's husband came creeping about, navigating his way around the dark quite easily, even though he reeked of alcohol. He seemed to be expecting a visit from his friend's eldest daughter, whistling and calling out to her salaciously. He paused at Nay's tree, his booze-addled mind confusing the satin cloth tied around the trunk for a playful sign from his mistress — and not the mark of a vengeful nang tani.

He looked around, trying to find the naive younger woman whom he had lied to, the woman who had fallen for his lecherous charms. As Nay's claws slashed at him from above, he realised, far too late, that he should've been looking up instead.

Over the next six months, Nay and Shao drove from villages to towns to cities, all across Thailand. Bamboo huts gave way to blocky apartment buildings, dirt paths led back to busy streets, but there were always banana trees, there were always husbands with selfish intentions — and there were always women who pleaded with Shao to help them deliver justice.

Eventually, Nay said goodbye to Thailand and Shao, thankful to her old friend for everything he'd shown her — and to the country for reminding her how swift her claws had once been, and why she had been called into existence in the first place.

Nay moved to Malaysia next, where another aspect of her was awakened: a pontianak named Melati. There, Melati travelled for another half a year to wherever she was needed, meeting toyols and penanggalans along the way, many of whom had been tiyanaks and manananggals in the Philippines. She met other pontianaks too — some of whom had always been in this form, while others had already lived hundreds of lifetimes, and would live hundreds more, all over Southeast Asia.

She made a brief stop in Indonesia after that — before deciding, however, that she still had unfinished business back in Singapore.

※ ※ ※

While having coffee along Orchard Road with one of her ex-colleagues — a rākṣasī named Tashny — Huang's email notification beeped. A second later, so did Tashny's. The pair looked at each other with knowing smiles, then checked their phones. The message was from a burner email address, and only contained a location — an abandoned two-storey building not far from town.

It was around six in the evening, but Tashny and Huang waited till the sun went down and the street lights along Orchard lit up, before taking a short bus ride and a walk together.

The abandoned building was filled with a variety of humans, spirits and creatures. Some of those humans looked like mystics and occultists and even warriors, while others looked like representatives of different beliefs from all around the world. Of the many spirits and creatures, Huang recognised most of them — but was certain that all of them were fellow former employees of The Company.

In the middle of the gathered crowd stood a pontianak named Tiqqy, The Company's former receptionist — and the one who had reached out to Melati while she was in Indonesia.

"We've all got different reasons to be here," Tiqqy said, her voice booming across the crowd, after expertly commanding their attention. "Some of you are here for vengeance. Some for self-preservation. Some are here because your beliefs compelled you to join our side. But we're all here for one common goal: to bring The Company down."

Huang held her head up high, the excitement in her growing as Tiqqy continued to speak, laying out plans and strategies for a number of assaults on The Company's office. When this was all over, Huang planned to return to Indonesia, where Melati would continue the work she was doing, the work she truly loved doing.

But before she could move on to be the best — and most complete — versions of herself, Huang owed it to the ba jiao gui aspect of her to raise her claws in defiance once more, in the land where she came into existence. She needed to prove — not to Belial and The Company — but to herself that the fault was never her own.

Work-Life Balance

Work-Life Balance

Isn't that...

...Zee's niece... Dina?

Wandering Spirit

If Mephistopheles is talking to her...

then that means...

You must be the new Senior Manager for Finance and Administration!

I didn't realise we had an *old* one.

I'm sure you *did*, Meph.

Work-Life Balance

Wandering Spirit

Thank you for your time today.

Work-Life Balance

Work-Life Balance

Wandering Spirit

Work-Life Balance

Work-Life Balance

It seems that a bit of *wandering* has done you well.

Thanks for inviting me, Shao.

I wasn't quite sure what I was going to do,

after *quitting* The Company.

It is *invigorating*,

to realise that there are other ways to *be* me.

That I'm not just a worker for The Company...

and that I'm not just tied to a single place.

Isn't it?

Wandering Spirit

Work-Life Balance

...our priests believe it will overload their *wards,*

and start a *cascading failure* enough to destroy the place.

The Company's presence would be set back by half a century, at least,

Goddess willing.

And **why** are you telling me this?

Work-Life Balance

Work-Life Balance

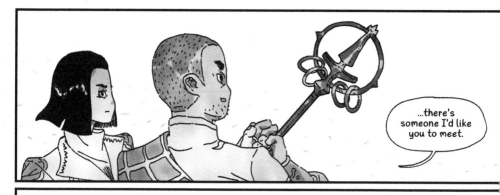

CHAPTER FOUR

Resignation

"As per my previous email," Dina typed furiously, "I'd triple-checked all details before forwarding the 16-3RΩ form to Belial. Belial was meant to simply approve the form, and not amend anything, before forwarding it to Leviathan's office. I have also attached the version of the form that Belial received, for everyone's perusal."

Dina leaned back into her ergonomically designed chair and stared intently at her screen for a moment. Her desk was empty except for her laptop, a tiny potted cactus that she'd named Mr Prickle, and a *Far Side* calendar whose pages hadn't been flipped since February. Dina leaned forward again, deleted the whole bit about Belial not needing to amend anything, added a 'Lord' in front of Leviathan's name, then signed off with a curt 'regards,' before hitting send.

It was three in the afternoon on a dreary Tuesday and Dina still hadn't had lunch. She knew that the basil pesto sandwich at the café over on Telok Ayer Street would've sold out already, but decided to give it a shot anyway.

Dina had hoped for an office before she joined The Company. Not necessarily a corner office, of course, but at the very least her own space. After all, she'd be entering as a Senior Manager of Finance and Administration, no small feat for someone at her age.

Her first day had started promisingly enough, with a helpful handover from her outgoing predecessor — an affable ba jiao gui named Xiao Huang, who sported a cute little retro eighties-inspired number. It took all of Dina's energy, however, to keep her smile from cracking when HR finally showed her to her desk later that day. It certainly wasn't an office — but, at the very least, she consoled herself, it was larger than the cubicle she'd had at her previous job. Besides, offices were reserved for the demons of the upper hierarchies.

Dina exhaled a heavy sigh as she stepped out of the building. She straightened her frumpy grey skirt, as her lanyard with her keycard attached at the end flapped awkwardly in the wind — tugging at the collar of her equally frumpy white blouse — then headed past Cecil Street, towards Telok Ayer.

Dina didn't mind slaying a minor demon every morning just to use the coffee machine. She had no problems with spilling a bit of her own blood to get the copier to work properly. She was even all right with the idea of not getting paid for overtime. What really made her blood boil was the boys' club mentality that plagued the upper hierarchies, from Belial on up.

It hadn't seemed so bad when she'd first joined. There were other creatures and spirits — like Tashny, the massive rākṣasī with the infectiously loud laugh, or Lita, the almost motherly manananggal she sometimes had lunch with — that shared a similar disdain for those upper hierarchies. As they all followed Huang's lead, however — one by one, replaced by humans who seemed happy to just keep their heads down — Dina started to feel more and more alone.

And it wasn't like the upper hierarchies were even particularly powerful when they existed on an earthly plane either — their abilities mostly limited to relatively small-scale illusions and deceptions — so even if they didn't like her, they certainly needed her. For that reason alone, she felt like she deserved their respect, if nothing else.

"Sorry, Dee," said Eric, the café's manager, from over the counter, just as Dina walked through the door. "We're all out of pesto." Dina exhaled another sigh, paid for her second choice — a smoked salmon sandwich — and a cappuccino, thanked Eric, and headed back to work.

When she returned to her cubicle, she told herself that she wouldn't check her inbox till she was done with lunch. She took a bite out of her sandwich and forced herself to stare at Mr Prickle as if he was the most compelling thing in the world. After she swallowed that first bite, she gave up, swivelled her chair to face her laptop, and opened her email.

"Hi Dina," the reply from Leviathan began. "While I appreciate your due diligence, I don't think this is a time to assign blame to—"

Dina closed her laptop, rubbed the bridge of her nose and sighed for the third time in less than half an hour, then continued to finish her late lunch, while trying to ignore the sounds of an intern's screams coming from the pantry.

❋ ❋ ❋

The dream always started by the stage at an indie club over on Upper Circular Road. Dina was with a couple of her secondary school friends. She was sixteen at the time. In her dream, her friends didn't have faces. Dina didn't see any sinister reason behind this; it's just that it had been so long since that night — since she even consciously thought about these friends — that she couldn't remember what any of them even looked like.

What she did clearly remember was clutching her electric violin close to her chest and how seemingly loud the rhythmic thumping of her heart was, like the beat of the preceding band's kick drum up on stage. "Oh god," Dina thought to herself in her dream. "We're going to be on stage!"

The club had an underaged night every Tuesday back then. Kids from all around Singapore would come by either to see their friends perform, or to have their first — and usually last — gigs. Dina was convinced that this wasn't going to happen to them though ("What were their names?"), that this wasn't going to be the end of their band ("Did we even have a band name?"), that this was only their first of many gigs.

Before she knew it, they were up on stage, performing their hearts out — an amateur-ish, but nevertheless competent, cover of a semi-popular pop-punk song. Everyone in the crowd was going wild, dancing and cheering with the kind of unrestrained enthusiasm that comes from that perfect marriage of youth and its unrivalled sense of freedom — everyone, except a colourfully dressed, older figure, smiling proudly in a corner.

Dina closed her eyes, breathing in the moment, focusing on her violin. But soon, she realised that the sounds of everything else had died down. She opened her eyes to see the crowd and her band frozen in a moment. Shocked, she let go of her violin, which continued playing without her.

She stared at it for a while — then realised that she didn't belong there. She walked off stage and looked around for the colourfully dressed figure to comfort her, but they were gone. Saddened, though not entirely surprised, Dina moved through the frozen crowd, and out the club's main entrance, the sound of her own violin fading behind her.

Normally, Dina would forget about this dream by the time she left her flat for work. She'd go through the first half of the day with an uneasy feeling, like there was something that she needed to get done, something she couldn't quite put her finger on. But, like the dream, that unease would fade eventually.

This morning, however, she woke to the sound of a violin playing. At first she thought she was imagining it, but as she tried to eat her unbuttered toast, while slipping on her shoes, she realised that the sound was coming from outside her flat. As Dina opened the door to leave, she saw a little girl in the flat opposite from hers — its door opened, but its gate shut. The girl was probably no more than ten years old, focusing intently on her music, moving her bow just the way she had practiced over and over again. She was good. A little bit stiff, but good.

Bach's *Air on the G String*. It had been one of Dina's favourites when she was that age.

Suddenly, she felt something grip her chest — a longing that she couldn't quite place. She wasn't sure what brought it about. She'd heard this piece countless times before, after all, long after she'd quit the band and the violin, long after she got caught up in her work life and in just... life.

Dina took a deep breath. She quietly closed her door, then paused for a moment, before marching a little too quickly towards the lift.

❉ ❉ ❉

"What a surprise," said Mephistopheles, knocking back his third beer of the evening. "Leviathan sided with the golden boy."

Every Wednesday after work, Dina and Mephistopheles would head to the fried chicken place over on Clarke Quay. They would order a bucket of hot wings that was meant for four people and tell the waitress to keep refreshing their drinks until eight-thirty, when they'd both head home — Dina to her rented flat in Hougang, Mephistopheles to the refurbished walk-up in Tiong Bahru that he managed to con a young couple out of, leading to their inevitable divorce.

"What d'ya think?" Dina slurred, angrily but with a hint of resignation, while wiping her lips with the sauce-stained back of her hand. "Every damn time. But when the right foreign leader doesn't get put into power or the plague of locusts hits the wrong village, who gets the blame then, huh? Who?" Dina let out a belch, took a sip of her fourth beer, then weakly added, as she slouched forward, "Every damn time…"

Mephistopheles was the only demon Dina got along with. Their Wednesday evening tradition had started after Dina was supposed to propose to Leviathan a more cost-efficient way for The Company to set up their own, seemingly legitimate religious organisations. Instead, Belial swooped in to take the lead — and the credit.

Mephistopheles offered to take her out for a drink, to cheer her up. She'd turned him down at first. Huang and a couple of others had given her nebulous warnings about him — he was a "shady" character and no one had been sure of his "intentions" — but Dina had a feeling that he was just… kind of lonely, really.

Still, she'd clumsily told him that she didn't go out with co-workers. He laughed for a solid ten seconds or so, before assuring her that he wasn't interested in her in that way. To prove his point, he said he'd bring her to a place that was guaranteed not to impress her.

He was right, of course. She did, however, appreciate the gesture.

Mephistopheles leaned over the back of his seat, waved to a waitress and mimed for the bill, then turned back to Dina and said, "I've been meaning to ask you something."

"Shoot," said Dina, pouting even as she made her bottle dance by tilting it left and right.

"Why The Company?"

Dina looked at her colleague, perplexed. "What do you mean?"

"I mean," said Mephistopheles, grabbing Dina's beer out of her hand and taking a swig, "we've done this for, like, three years now, and every single time, you've got something new to complain about."

"Hey," Dina interrupted, weakly wrestling her drink away from Mephistopheles. "Rude."

Mephistopheles almost immediately snatched the beer back. "Oh please. You're not gonna finish it and it's only getting warmer."

"That's..." she started, defensively at first, then slouching back down, continued, "Yeah, okay, that's fair."

"And don't change the subject," continued Mephistopheles. "It's never a small thing with these guys. You very clearly hate it here. So, why don't you quit and work for someone less... well, evil?"

"Pfft. As if companies with morals could afford dental."

Mephistopheles rolled his eyes. "Fine, don't talk about it."

"Look, man," Dina said, casually. "I don't see what the big deal is. Sure, I complain constantly, but who doesn't hate their job?"

"Not everyone's job is helping to bring about the end of the world though. Don't you feel anything for the rest of your people?"

"No," Dina said, so flatly that it shocked Mephistopheles a little. "Not really," she added when she noticed how uncomfortable he was.

"What happened?" the demon asked.

Dina fought through her booze-addled haze and sobered up enough to focus. "Nothing," said Dina, conspicuously turning away from her colleague for just a second too long. "I started working in this line 'cause I needed the money. I kept working 'cause I was good at it. In the meantime, everything and everyone outside of work that I cared about just kind of... gradually fell to the wayside or disappointed me, y'know? So, no. I really don't care about the 'rest of my people.'"

For a moment, it seemed like everything went silent in the restaurant. Mephistopheles frowned at Dina, clearly wanting to say something, but as Dina shifted restlessly in her chair, the waitress arrived with the bill, and the loud noise and furious activity returned. Mephistopheles handed the waitress a couple of notes and told her to keep the change.

"I'm sorry," he finally said to Dina, with a weight behind his words that seemed heavier than necessary.

Dina sat upright and smiled at her friend. "It's fine, man. Really. But the next time you do a coffee run for Belial and his boys, just do me a favour and spit in his."

Mephistopheles grinned deviously. "What makes you think I don't already?"

❈ ❈ ❈

"Dear all," read the email from Nergal, The Company's Chief of Security, "there's currently an infestation in the foyer. While the tartaruchi and I are handling the situation, I would advise all personnel to work off-site, at least for the morning. We will provide you with an update by noon."

Dina was already two stations away from the office when she received the email. She went through her mental rolodex of what needed to be done that day, weighed that against her own recent frustrations with Belial, and decided that, yeah, she deserved a work-from-home day. She alighted at the next station, walked up to street level and waited for a bus that would take her on a long ride home.

An "infestation", Dina knew, was code for an attack on The Company from what was internally referred to as The Competition — a collection of soldiers, occultists and earthly agents, as well as a couple of creatures and spirits. No one outside of the building would be panicking over the full-blown siege though. The tartaruchi could cloud the minds of passers-by, as long as the attack remained within the foyer. Which it would, since nothing short of a keycard would allow them to advance any further.

Dina hopped onto her bus as it arrived and felt herself ease up as she melted into her seat's cushion. As the bus took turn after turn, she shut her eyes and bathed in the warmth of the morning's light filtering in through the windows, suddenly realising that she hadn't enjoyed this much sun in quite a while.

The kid was playing her violin again. Dina could hear it as soon as she alighted the lift on her floor. *Air on the G String.*

As she started to unlock her gate, Dina realised that the kid had stopped and that she wasn't alone anymore. "Zohra, honey," said a woman in a nurse's uniform, squatting down next to the girl. Her mother, Dina presumed. "Enough violin for this morning, all right? Time for breakfast. Amma's already late for work."

The child, Zohra, was about to head into the kitchen and out of Dina's line of sight, when, before she could stop herself, Dina blurted out, "Hey! Sorry..."

Zohra's mother turned towards Dina, a defensive look briefly passing across her face, before she put on her mask of civility. "Yes?" she said.

"Sorry, I just..." Dina realised at that moment that she wasn't sure where she was going with this, but the longing in her chest had returned and was practically screaming at her to say something. So, she let herself go, let herself just speak. "The way you're gripping your violin — Zohra, is it? — I can tell, even from here, that it's a little tight. I used to do that too. My teacher told me off constantly! Just loosen it a little. Don't worry, you're not going to lose control. Quite the opposite actually..."

Zohra's mother glared at Dina, clearly going through a list of responses she had ready for nosy neighbours. Zohra, however, silently stared at Dina through the flat's locked gate, as she loosened her grip and started playing again.

Zohra's mother turned her attention back to her daughter, whose eyes had lit up. Both of them could clearly hear the difference. Zohra's mother's expression softened and, after a moment, she turned back to Dina. "Her teacher could never figure that out."

"I'm sure she would've at some point," Dina said.

"We had to stop her lessons. I'm already working a double-shift twice a week and her piece-of-shit father—"

"Amma!" Zohra said, interrupting her playing.

"Sorry," her mother said, smiling at Dina. "Her deadbeat dad?" She paused, waiting for Zohra's approval, which the little girl delivered with a nod, before she started playing again. "Her deadbeat dad can't be trusted to pay his share."

"That sucks," said Dina.

"Yeah," agreed Zohra's mother, then added, "I'm Priya, by the way."

"Dina."

"Are you a music teacher, by any chance, Dina?"

"Nah, but I loved the violin when I was a kid."

"Why'd you stop?"

Dina paused for a moment. "Life, I guess?"

"That's a dumbass—"

"Amma!" interjected Zohra again.

"That's a dumb excuse, if you ask me," corrected Priya with a smile, as her daughter continued playing.

"Is it though?" said Dina, more defensively than she had expected. She continued, more conversationally this time, "I mean, I'm sure you understand. There's always work to worry about. I have to live my life."

"You call that living?"

"Well... yeah," she said, that longing suddenly gripping her chest tighter than ever before.

"And that's enough then? Nothing else to care for — to be passionate about — but work?"

"Yeah," said Dina, forcing a tone of certainty. "Yeah, it is."

"Then why'd you help Zohra?"

Dina opened her mouth, ready to respond, but couldn't find the answer to the question. She did, however, finally understand what that longing in her chest was. Priya smiled and left Dina with her thoughts, as she silently gestured for Zohra to head to the kitchen.

❄ ❄ ❄

Dina's Titi Zee had suggested that they meet for coffee in the mall that had been built over the old Seletar Estate. She wasn't sure why they'd picked this place specifically — it was pretty out of the way for both of them — but she was mostly just surprised that they'd even answered her call at all.

Dina had only seen Titi Zee on and off when she was much younger — something about their work — but after they'd returned into her life, the pair became inseparable. They'd take her out for ice cream when she was seven, they'd listened intently as she talked about girls when she was fourteen, and they encouraged her music all throughout — at least until they disappeared again about ten years ago.

Dina secretly hoped that Titi Zee wouldn't take her call. She didn't want to talk to them, but she knew that if there was anyone she should speak with about that longing in her chest, it was them.

She'd planned to keep her tone level and her expression neutral, but the moment she saw them — their dark brown face heavier with lines, but their purple batik shirt and bright green sarong as colourful as ever — she ran straight into their arms like she was a kid again.

"I've missed you," Dina said, her voice shaking as they took a seat at a half-filled coffee place, one of those that attempted to approximate old-time decor with a modern twist. "Where the hell have you been?" she continued, still managing to hold back her tears, even as the disappointment that she'd learned to keep in check for years tainted every word.

"I..." Zee started, but faltered as they started to tear up. "Do you remember what I used to tell you about your grandfather?"

Dina wanted to yell at them. She didn't want to talk about the rest of their family. She needed answers from them — answers that would help her figure out what to do next. Instead, she composed herself and curtly replied, "Yes," followed by a slightly warmer, "You... said he was a bad man."

Zee nodded, then continued, "I had escaped your grandfather's shadow when I was younger, but doing so meant... that there was more work to be done."

Dina couldn't help but let out a mirthless laugh. "More work. Just like when I was a kid. I swear, I take after you in that way."

"I know. That's why you called me, isn't it?" Zee said.

Dina shook her head, her frustration growing. "What are you—" She stopped suddenly, that frustration replaced by realisation. "How did you...?" She looked around the coffee place, and there, among the moderately sized crowd, she saw them.

Huang, the ba jiao gui, sat at the table just behind Titi Zee. At another, nearby table, Tashny, the rākṣasī, and Lita, the manananggal, sipped their own drinks.

The Competition.

"I..." she said, all the anger finally fading away. "I guess I always knew... knew what you did."

"But you didn't know about The Company," Zee said, their tone laced with anger — but not at her. "And I was too lost in my work to notice that we'd lost you to them."

"You didn't lose me," Dina said, defeated. "I just stopped caring after you left again, and they were there to fill that hole."

Zee sighed sadly, and took Dina's hands in theirs. "I'm not saying what I did was right. I shouldn't have disappeared again, no matter how important I felt my work was. And I understand that, for whatever reasons, it's easy to let your life fall under the shadow of others. Believe me, I understand." Zee moved their hands to Dina's face, and Dina finally felt tears well up in her eyes. "Do whatever you do next, not because of or for me, not even because of what The Company is. After all this time, do it — just for you, sayang."

Dina sat quietly for a moment, sobbing softly, then looked up at her Titi and smiled, that longing in her chest disappearing — forever.

Work-Life Balance

Resignation

Work-Life Balance

Thank you! And, oh...

...careful!

Eep! It's heavy.

Belial was chasing me all week for those reports.

Make sure he gets them soon.

Before that...

Work-Life Balance

Resignation

Work-Life Balance

We meet again.

Good luck dealing with the **higher-ups.**

You'll need it.

Yo
too

Good luck, wherever you are going.

Work-Life Balance

Resignation

❋ ❋ ❋

"Where's the mouthy human this morning?" asked Belial two weeks later as he walked past Dina's cubicle, less out of concern and more out of yet another opportunity to win some favour with Leviathan.

"Don't know," scoffed Mammon. "She's left her laptop here too. Must be sick, I guess. You know how fragile these puny little humans are."

The pair cackled a little. "Well," said Belial, "we could always—" He stopped suddenly when he noticed that there was another conspicuously empty cubicle that day. "Wait... where's Mephistopheles?" he asked.

Resignation

Work-Life Balance

Work-Life Balance

❄ ❄ ❄

Dina had told Mephistopheles not to go into the office that day, to run and take only what he needed with him. But he had something he needed to pick up from the office first — a ledger that never seemed to run out of pages.

The ledger was a little beat-up, but otherwise pretty well maintained. All accounts on its pages were written in red. Before he had fallen out with the upper hierarchies a long, long time ago, Mephistopheles was as close to a free agent that a demon could be. He liked that life — and he felt that he could finally live it to its fullest, now more than ever.

He didn't tell Dina, or The Competition, about the ledger. He promised her that he would be better — that he would show Huang, Tashny, Lita and all the rest that he was who she said he was, not who they thought he was.

He didn't say when he'd start though. He liked Dina, he really did. But, as he snuck out of the office early that morning, he chuckled to himself deviously — though not at all maliciously.

He was a demon, after all.

And humans never read the fine print.

Work-Life Balance

The tartaruchi are killing us!

Will the *hantu raya* be coming?

Sabar lah, kena pujuk ni.

Okay, dah!

!?

Work-Life Balance

Nergal...!

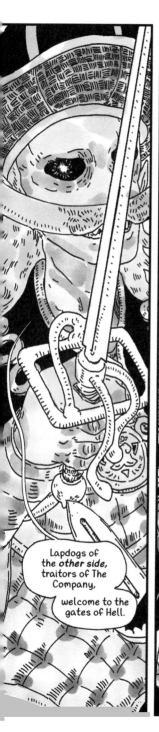

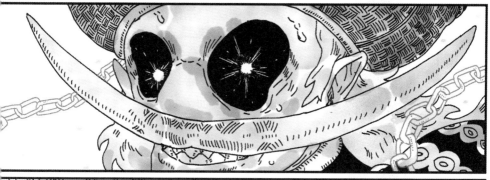

This new siege could not be hidden by Nergal and the tartaruchi. The Competition — its ranks greater than ever — stormed the foyer and, thanks to the keycard they had procured from Dina a week ago, they managed to make their way to the upper levels with the noise of thunder, a noise that made sure that everyone downtown came to see.

Work-Life Balance

And they...

Work-Life Balance

...most certainly saw.

※ ※ ※

In Hougang, however, Dina was blissfully unaware of precisely what was happening at the office. Nor did she care. Her only concern at that very moment was that Mr Prickle seemed to be adjusting quite well to his new home.

She looked up at the clock in her bedroom and saw that it was close to ten, so she stepped over to her desk and popped open a beat-up violin case. She'd picked up the instrument from a second-hand store earlier that week. She cradled it in the groove of her collarbone, then adjusted it a little till it felt right.

The doorbell rang. Priya had said that she couldn't pay Dina, but Dina had told her that wasn't the point. "Besides," she said, "I'd saved up quite a bit from my last job, so it's not like I'll starve." She opened the door, saw the look of excitement on Zohra's face and, suddenly, Dina remembered what her secondary school friends looked like, what every single person in the crowd that night felt. And she knew that this was right where she belonged.

Zohra and Dina waved goodbye to Priya. "All right," said Dina, as she closed the door. "Let's work a little more on *Air* this morning and see what else we can do, yeah?"

EPILOGUE

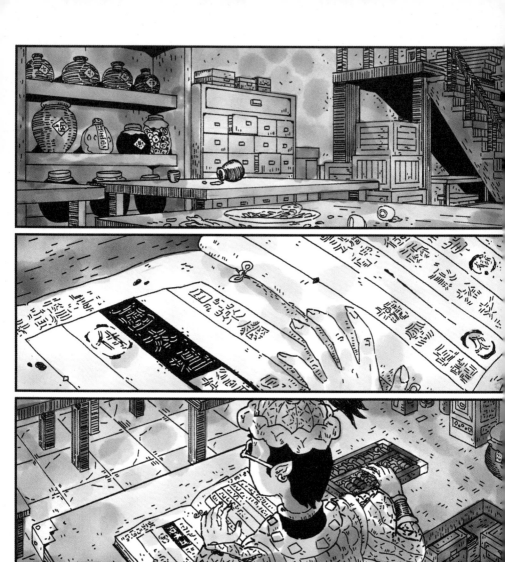

Work-Life Balance

"This fight was never about winners or losers. It has been, and always will be, about..."

※ ※ ※

MEPHISTOPHELES'S INHUMAN RESOURCES

Navigating the creatures and spirits within this region has been challenging.

Even within different countries, there are all these cultures and customs. I thought maybe the legends I'd managed to glean about them could help, but it turns out that those legends are... well, just that: myths, built by the humans around half-truths and stories.

Granted, my new colleagues already hate my guts and no amount of anthropological knowledge is going to help that, but I'm hoping this little cheat sheet of my co-workers and the region's other folkloric freelancers will at least make it easier for me to understand them.

PONTIANAKS

Probably the most common spirits around this region, pontianaks have been feared by humans for at least three centuries. Apparently, there's a whole city named after them, so they're clearly a formidable bunch.

WHAT I'VE HEARD

Pontianaks usually dwell within banana trees. They're often described as "vampiric", but have been generally known to disembowel their victims and feed on their guts. They tend to favour white dresses to match their pale complexions, and wear their long hair plainly. Some legends claim they're vengeful spirits of women who've died in childbirth, but this varies depending on the country.

WHAT I'VE LEARNED

The understanding of pontianak fashion might be just a little out of date. Tiqqy, for example, seems effortlessly stylish and sometimes even sports a bob cut. I'm sure she's feasted on blood and entrails in her day, but I've mostly seen her go for iced coffee and burgers.

MANANANGGALS

Manananggals are known for severing their torsos from the lower half of their bodies, then flying around at night on wings that extend from their shoulder blades.

WHAT I'VE HEARD

According to popular accounts, manananggals' wings somewhat resemble those of my ilk's: leathery and expansive. Pregnant women and their unborn children, husbands who've left their wives, happy couples — no one can agree on who exactly their victims of choice are, but most folks seem certain that these creatures feed on unsuspecting humans by sucking their blood with a proboscis-like tongue.

WHAT I'VE LEARNED

After speaking with Lita a couple of times, I can confirm that manananggals use their tongues to attack — though it's less to suck blood and more to cut you down with their words. Their wings aren't so much leathery as they are extensions of their flesh. Before joining The Company, Lita was more inclined to prey on philandering or abusive men than anyone else.

BA JIAO GUIS

Ba jiao guis offer up lucky lottery numbers or some other means of financial aid when summoned. They only retaliate when humans rescind their end of the bargain — which, unsurprisingly, happens a lot.

WHAT I'VE HEARD

Like pontianaks, ba jiao guis live in banana trees. (The direct translation of "ba jiao gui" is "banana ghost".) They can be summoned by tying a red string to their tree and sticking needles into its trunk. The details of how they exact their revenge on greedy humans are sketchy, though I suspect that's intentional. After all, that just means that any questionable death of someone with a gambling problem can be chalked up to one of their kind.

WHAT I'VE LEARNED

A ba jiao gui like Xiao Huang can be summoned with string and needles, sure — but she responds just as quickly to an email that's marked "urgent". They're sentimental spirits, which I guess goes hand in hand with their ever-optimistic hope that humans' better natures will prevail.

RĀKṢASĪS

One of the oldest creatures in this region, the rākṣasīs have been around for millenia. Because of that long history, all sorts of stories about them have sprung forth from numerous cultures and religions.

WHAT I'VE HEARD

There are tonnes of different legends and myths surrounding the rākṣasīs, but the most common one I've heard — and mind you, this is a huge oversimplification — is that they're a little like trolls: massive creatures with monstrous fangs, and a taste for human blood that they'll guzzle out from their victims' skulls. Depending on who you ask, they're either forest-dwelling beasts that terrorise anyone that crosses their paths, or proud warriors that were part of many epic battles — or both.

WHAT I'VE LEARNED

One look at Tashny and you can tell that the legends about the rākṣasīs' impressive size certainly haven't been exaggerated. Proud warriors? I don't know about that, but if the much-deserved beating she gave Belial when they first met is any indication, she can definitely handle herself in a fight.

KUCHISAKE-ONNAS

Kuchisake-onnas (or slit-mouthed women) are a kind of onryō, a broad term for vengeful spirits from Japan. Traditionally, one way to spot these spirits was to pay close attention to how they wore their kimonos; onryōs always have the right side folded over the left.

WHAT I'VE HEARD

This particular onryō has scabbed-over slits stretching from her lips to the middle of her cheeks. She'll ask her victims if they think she's pretty and, depending on their response, she'll either stab them or slice up their faces.

WHAT I'VE LEARNED

Asuka, the kuchisake-onna who transferred over to our local office, seems less interested in soliciting compliments, and more concerned with updating our filing systems. In fact, she sometimes wears a mask, and I'm guessing that habit stems as much out of shyness as it does from her native culture's courteous concerns over hygiene.

NANG TANIS

Nang tanis also dwell within banana trees. (What is up with banana trees in this region?)

WHAT I'VE HEARD

Nang tanis are said to be generally benevolent. Most stories about them focus on how they'll offer food to travel-weary monks. There are, however, some accounts of them slaying lecherous men. They've got green complexions, which I guess is to blend in with their surroundings, and they usually hover just a little off the ground.

WHAT I'VE LEARNED

Not much. There isn't a nang tani on the local office's payroll, but I wanted to read up on them, just in case that changes.

TOYOLS

Toyols seem to be just as common around this region as pontianaks. The biggest difference, however, is that toyols are more mischievous than menacing, working as little helpers for anyone that summons them.

WHAT I'VE HEARD

Toyols are undead infants that're used by humans to steal or sabotage. Keeping one entails the same kind of work as looking after an actual human child... more or less. You feed them treats and milk, you give them toys to play with, you chant incantations, and you offer up a bit of blood.

WHAT I'VE LEARNED

The myths and the reality are pretty similar, but rather than wreaking havoc, The Company's toyols — like that eager little guy, Othman — handle day-to-day admin instead.

Clocking in Overtime

A LOOK BEHIND THE SCENES OF
WORK-LIFE BALANCE

WAYNE RÉE : How Ben and I worked together was pretty simple: we both did our own thing. Okay, there's more to it than that, but that's certainly the first part of it.

After I wrote each prose piece, Ben took a look at it. He planned how he'd either interpret the story or build upon it. More than a couple of times, he shared some thoughts that really helped my stories too.

Once all the prose pieces were done, Ben thumbnailed his complementing comic. We'd then go through the thumbnails together and see where we could tighten up the connections between our stories, either in the prose universe or the comics universe, while still allowing enough room for each to be its own thing. Ben would then start pencilling, while our editor extraordinaire, Shreya, shared her own thoughts on the stories, on how we could make the comics and prose flow even more seamlessly into and around each other, and on how terrible my typos were.

WAYNE RÉE : I'm not an idiot. When it came to visual storytelling and character designs, I got the hell out of Ben's way. I'd share my thoughts if he asked, but I mean, come on. Look at these exploratory drawings!

BENJAMIN CHEE : I tried to find scenes that I could latch onto visually as I read through Wayne's stories, then reimagined them in the setting of the comic. As I explored those ideas, they tended to become starting points for the comic interpretations. One of my favourite scenes is of the women having lunch, and while this drawing didn't make it into the comic, it definitely informed us about the camaraderie they share, and they became more involved in the story.

BENJAMIN CHEE : Another favourite is Zee having Tashny the rākṣasī toss out Belial and Mammon. It's just a short line, but expanded upon in drawing, it's a scene that could tell you much more. (left page)

I loved how Mephistopheles quietly makes his exit, but I also think he'd relish the opportunity to make his distaste known, if given the chance. (above)

BENJAMIN CHEE : I was taught to begin with the background characters when attempting to build a setting. "Resignation" was actually the first piece Wayne wrote, so that was where we started from: the soldiers of The Company and The Competition. Between them, there's a rich range of costumes that would later inform what might look good on Zee, Dina, Lita, Tashny et al.

WAYNE RÉE : One of the great things about seeing Ben's exploratory drawings early in the process is that they informed how the other prose stories were written. The style affected the characters' tone a little, which made it easier to tie the prose universe and the comics universe together.

Playing Politics

CREATING AN ACCOMPANYING GAME
FOR WORK-LIFE BALANCE

WAYNE RÉE : *Internal Damnation* is a standalone text-based game set in *Work-Life Balance*'s prose universe. It was created by Ben and myself; the Difference Engine team; developers, Lionfish Studios; and game audio studio, Imba Interactive. The game focuses on an intern's time in The Company and takes place somewhere around the middle of "Resignation".

When Difference Engine first suggested creating this, I very confidently said, "Yeah, sure!" Which is hilarious 'cause the last time I regularly played anything digitally, the PlayStation 2 was the most popular console around. I do, however, love gamebooks, and I helped out with Victor Fernando R. Ocampo's email-based interactive story, *The Book of Red Shadows*. So, I at least knew enough to get started.

I began with an online tool called Twine to map out all the different choices the reader could take. This was as much for Lionfish Studios to get an idea of what we were coming up with, as it was for my own clarity.

After that, I fleshed out the story, which was a unique challenge in itself. While I had the different paths mapped out, it was hard to keep the main character's motivations straight, depending on which path was chosen. Thankfully, Shreya and the team helped to keep the emotional beats consistent.

WAYNE RÉE : Ben and I thought that his isometric style would work great for the game's visuals, but we figured that we could use it for the book's cover too. It's incredibly striking, and it perfectly captures what we're doing with the comics and the prose. As soon as I felt more confident with the game's story, Ben and I discussed what the new characters would look like, how the characters from the book would translate in the game, and what the environments would look like.

BENJAMIN CHEE : To begin, Wayne put together a table that lists the maximum amount of characters needed at a location at one time, so each of the locations can be designed to accommodate just that. After that, I thought of how they might be connected to each other in the game, as well as presented together in the wimmelbild-esque cover art.

CHAPTER 666:
OFFICE CULTURE & HELPFUL HINTS

Ensure proper email etiquette.
If you don't misuse the word "revert" at least once a week, you may face disciplinary action.

Interns are always welcome!
Anyone can devour souls, but it takes care and dedication to crush them. Direct any interested parties to **wlbgame.differenceengine.sg**

In case of fire, use the lifts.
The Company appreciates your sacrifice! (Do ensure that your timesheets are updated before sacrificing yourself though.)

ABOUT THE CREATORS

WAYNE RÉE wrote the prose for *Work-Life Balance*.

He's the co-creator of the comic *Worlds Apart: A Conversation About Mental Health* (with Nurjannah Suhaimi), and the fan favourite audio series *Ghost Maps* (with Kyle Ong).

His short stories have appeared in *LONTAR: The Journal of Southeast Asian Speculative Fiction, Infinite Worlds Magazine, The Epigram Books Collection of Best New Singaporean Short Stories,* and *Fish Eats Lion Redux.*

He first collaborated with Benjamin Chee on *Mr Memphis.*

His least favourite job ever was when he worked as a social media manager. His favourite job ever was when he worked as a night-shift security guard.

Find him online at **www.waynereewrites.com**

❀ ❀ ❀

BENJAMIN CHEE created the comics and illustrations for *Work-Life Balance.*

He enjoys mashing up genres and themes, so after making several books with titles like *Charsiew Space* and *Lychee Queen*, he ended up asking Wayne Rée for permission to adapt the wild west short story, *Mr Memphis*, into a wuxia comic... leading to them making this book together.

His comics are collected in *Liquid City Volume 3, Asian Monsters,* and *SOUND: A Comics Anthology.*

He is terrified of horror movies and hasn't yet fully comprehended why he is part of this book with its abundance of hantu.

Find him online at **www.charsiewspace.com**

ACKNOWLEDGEMENTS

Thank you, of course, to Ben, for being a great collaborator, friend, and appreciator of fried chicken. And thank you to the Difference Engine team. This book could never have been what it is without you guys.

To Meihan, Paolo, Paul, and all the other creators who shared your incredibly kind words (as well as a shout-out to Tina, for your help).

To my work-wife, Kyle, for your support and Southeast Asian supernatural knowledge. Huat ah!

To Jenn and Shilt, for providing a space for me to work on this book.

To Audrey, Chris, Donna, Joline, and Leia, for all the movies, makan, and game nights.

To Jo and Max, and Jerry and Anna, for rolling along with us.

To Priya and Zohra, Rubyni, Shao, Tashny, and Tiqqy, for allowing me to use your names.

To Asuka, not only for allowing me to name a demon after you, but also for your advice. Also, to Nazry, for your feedback, and to Aditi, for the proofreading.

And, of course, to Nadia — for how well we balance each other.

— **WAYNE RÉE**

❄ ❄ ❄

Thank you, Wayne, for once again trusting me with your stories, and the Difference Engine team, for putting all the pieces together.

The dialogue font used in the comics is Pretzel, designed by Sara Linsley.

Drawing, for me, has been largely a solitary process, made doubly so by circumstances during the pandemic. I appreciated all you lovely people who made time to keep me company, feed me, and provide necessary motivation, online and off.

Special thanks to my air fryer, which has cooked me many meals over the course of creating this book.

Lastly, to you, the reader, I hope you enjoyed this two-track journey along with Zee, Xiao Huang, Dina, and company. May you find the balance that works for your life.

— **BENJAMIN CHEE**